Class Trip to the Haunted House

Find out more spooky secrets about

Ghostville Elementary®

Ghostville Elementary®

Class Trip to the Haunted House

by Marcia Thornton Jones
and
Debbie Dadey

illustrated by Guy Francis

A
LITTLE APPLE
PAPERBACK

SCHOLASTIC INC.
New York   Toronto   London   Auckland   Sydney
Mexico City   New Delhi   Hong Kong   Buenos Aires

ISBN 0-439-67809-9

12 11 10 9 8 7 6 5 4   6 7 8 9 10/0

Printed in the U.S.A.   40
First printing, February 2005

To Lynne S. Brandon — a real treasure!
— MTJ

To my wonderful youngest son,
Alex Dadey
— DD

Contents

THE LEGEND

*Sleepy Hollow Elementary School's
Online Newspaper*

**This Just In: D and D time spells Dread and Doom
for Ghostville Elementary!**

Breaking News: The third graders in the basement are trying to work out problems during D and D time. According to their teacher, D and D stands for Debate and Drama. If you ask this reporter, it's more like Dread and Doom time for the poor kids in the basement. I sincerely doubt anything can save the third graders from the ghosts haunting their room. Not even finding the legendary Blackburn treasure!

Your friendly fifth-grade reporter,
Justin Thyme

1
D and D

"Me first!" Andrew rushed to the front of the classroom when Mr. Morton announced D and D time. Immediately a ghost popped out of a crack in the wall.

Ozzy had been the reigning bully in the basement of Sleepy Hollow for more than 100 years, so he wasn't too happy about Andrew taking over as the newest troublemaker in the third-grade classroom.

When Andrew opened his mouth to speak, Ozzy blew on the old tray beneath the chalkboard. A cloud of dust swirled around Andrew's head.

"*Ahhh-CHOOOOO!*" Andrew sneezed, then wiped his nose on the sleeve of his T-shirt.

Of course, Andrew couldn't see or hear Ozzy or the rest of the ghosts in the basement room. Ghosts were like that. They decided who could see them, and so far they had picked only three kids: Jeff, Cassidy, and Nina.

Cassidy shook her head at Ozzy, trying to get him to stop. Nina closed her dark eyes and sighed. Jeff grinned. It suited him just fine that Ozzy was pestering Andrew.

"My family is moving!" Andrew announced.

"Yay!" Jeff cheered. A classroom without Andrew sounded perfect — even if that classroom was haunted by troublesome ghosts from more than 100 years ago. Jeff would take the ghosts over Andrew any day.

Mr. Morton gave Jeff a warning glance. Their third-grade teacher had been doing that a lot lately. Especially since he'd come up with his newest idea: Debate and Drama time.

"Debate and drama are two great ways for us to work out any differences we might have," Mr. Morton had announced. "We'll spend the last fifteen minutes of each day taking turns talking about what's important to us. Then we can discuss and act out ways of solving problems."

Most kids liked the idea until Jeff and Andrew started competing for D and D time. Jeff thought he should be center stage every day since he wanted to make movies. Andrew, on the other hand, could talk about absolutely nothing for fifteen minutes without taking a breath, just like now.

Andrew didn't bat an eye when Jeff cheered. "I'm not moving away," Andrew said. "I'll still be living in Sleepy Hollow and going to school here."

"Rats," Jeff muttered and slid down in his seat until his chin rested on his old-fashioned desk.

Jeff wasn't the only one who was disappointed. Green glitter swirled in the air above Andrew's head. The glitter turned to haze and transformed into another ghost: Sadie.

Sadie was not known for laughing and having fun, but when Andrew made his announcement, Sadie *really* started to bawl. Giant tears slid down her transparent cheeks and plopped on Andrew's head. Andrew looked up, but he could only see cobwebs hanging from the lights.

"In fact" — Andrew puffed out his chest and went into full bragging mode — "my family is moving into the biggest house in town."

"That would be the Blackburn Estate," Nina gasped.

Nina, Cassidy, and Jeff had gone to a

moving sale at the Blackburn Estate. The caretaker had given them an old fiddle and a cracked dish to use as props in their class play. Later, the kids discovered that two more ghosts had followed them back to school, hidden inside the fiddle and dish — Calliope and her black cat, Cocomo.

"Exactly," Andrew said. "My mother just inherited so much money that I'll be the richest kid in town."

"But the Blackburn Estate is falling apart," Cassidy blurted out. "Why would you want to live there?"

"My dad plans on turning the Blackburn Estate into the biggest and bestest mansion this side of the Mississippi," Andrew said. "Dad's going to tear most of it down and rebuild it."

At his words, a scream ripped through the air and echoed down the halls, bringing the class to a dead stop.

2
A Screeching Halt

Usually Cassidy, Jeff, and Nina didn't see Calliope the ghost very much, except when she played her violin and sang songs with notes that didn't quite match. But when they heard the scream, they knew exactly which ghost it was coming from. Calliope's scream was as off-key as her singing. It ripped through the air and bounced off the walls. It rattled the windows and made Ozzy jump so high his head went through the ceiling.

Nina put her fingers in her ears. Cassidy yelped. Jeff fell out of his chair.

Jeff knew it took tremendous ghost energy — and something very important — to break the ghost-sound barrier so that everyone could hear. Calliope's scream did just that.

The entire class erupted in shouts and squeals. A girl named Carla jumped up from her seat in the front row.

"Is somebody . . ."

". . . hurt?" her twin sister, Darla, finished.

Mr. Morton pushed back his chair so fast it toppled over. "Stay in your seats," Mr. Morton yelled over his shoulder as he rushed into the hallway to see if someone needed help.

Five kids hopped up and followed Mr. Morton. Three more kids swung open the back door that led straight outside to the playground.

"Hey!" Andrew shouted. "Where's everybody going? I was in the middle of my story. I haven't gotten to the part about how much this is going to cost. You'll never believe it! Come back here!"

"It looks like your story has come to a *screeching* halt," Jeff said with a satisfied grin. "As soon as Mr. Morton comes back, it'll be my turn."

Andrew curled his fingers into a fist. "This is your fault, isn't it?" he asked. "You used some movie special effect to interrupt me before I got to the best part."

Jeff's lifetime goal was to be a movie producer, and everybody knew he practiced by making his own videos. "I didn't do anything," Jeff said.

"It had to be you," Andrew said, taking a step toward Jeff.

Carla moved between them. "You'd

9

better stop fighting. D and D time is supposed to be for working out our problems . . ."

". . . not for starting fights," Darla finished the warning.

No sooner were the words out of their mouths than Calliope the musical ghost floated down the aisle between Nina and Cassidy.

Calliope's long dark braid floated above her head. Her cat, Cocomo, reached up to swat at Calliope's dress, but the ghostly claws went right through the flowing fabric.

Calliope gazed straight ahead as if she didn't see anything else in the room. She looked different than usual. Her body had turned a sickly shade of yellow and her eyes glowed green like mushy peas.

The rest of the ghosts noticed, too. They hurried out of Calliope's way, going straight through desks and chairs. Calliope stopped next to Andrew in the front of the room. Andrew didn't have a clue that a ghost had appeared next to him.

Calliope opened her mouth to speak, but nothing came out. Her eyes grew big and the yellow of her skin deepened to the color of a rotten banana. Her green eyes watered like a swamp, but she didn't cry.

Again, she opened her mouth to speak. Not a single word came out. It was as if somebody, or something, had silenced Calliope forever.

3
Scared Speechless

Every day after Calliope lost her voice, exactly fifteen minutes before the end of school, she made her way to the front of the room. It didn't matter if Andrew or Jeff or any other student was already standing there for D and D.

Calliope stood dead center and opened her mouth as if she had something to say, but no words came out.

"What is wrong with her?" Cassidy whispered to Nina. "She's been doing this for a week."

Nina shrugged and pretended to listen to Carla tell how she hated when people wasted paper. Out of the side of her mouth, Nina admitted, "Calliope's getting on my nerves."

"Whatever's bothering her," Jeff said

from behind them, "must be important and very scary."

The three friends nodded. What could be so bad that it scared Calliope speechless? Even the other ghosts were worried. They crowded around Calliope as if they were trying to help her. The front of the classroom looked like a ghost traffic jam.

Ozzy's ghost dog, Huxley, howled, and so did Ozzy. His sister, Becky, frowned so much that her face drooped. Sadie cried so many tears, a puddle formed on the floor. Jeff hoped nobody slipped on the wet spot.

Finally, Carla finished talking and Andrew dashed to the front of the room before Jeff could raise his hand. Calliope opened her mouth as if to scream. She shook her head back and forth, her long hair whipping through the air. Of course, no sound came from her. Calliope was still speechless.

"I wish we could help Calliope," Nina said. "Even Cocomo is upset." When Andrew bragged about the Blackburn Estate, Calliope's cat arched her back and her claws came out.

"My room is going to be at the top of a turret," Andrew explained. "That's one of those round towers. It's painted pink right now, but Mom said I can paint it camouflage colors."

That just made Cocomo angrier. She tried to shred Andrew's jeans, but her claws moved right through his leg. Andrew shivered and batted at his knees as if a gnat had landed there.

"Andrew hogs all the D and D time talking about the Blackburn Estate," Jeff complained under his breath to his friends.

"Forget about Andrew," Nina said softly. "We should worry about Calliope."

Cassidy nodded. "If we don't help her soon, there's no telling what she'll do next."

4
Worst Bully

After school that day, Jeff took his time stuffing his homework into his backpack.

"What's taking you so long?" Cassidy asked.

"Hurry up," Nina told him. "Everyone else has left already. You act like you want to stay at school all night."

"I think you're right, Nina," Jeff said. "You said we should get to the bottom of Calliope's problem. Well, you convinced me. That's exactly what we need to do."

"I thought you only cared about Andrew and his bragging," Cassidy said.

"Andrew IS driving me crazy," Jeff admitted. "If he doesn't stop stealing all the D and D time, I'm going to scream."

A green haze swirled around Jeff. Ozzy appeared with his nose less than an inch away from Jeff's. "I don't like that Andrew, either," Ozzy snapped. "Let's knock the snot out of him!"

"You can't do that!" Nina shrieked.

Ozzy pounded one fist into the other. "If I concentrate hard enough, I could smack Andrew right across his kisser."

"No," Cassidy said. "What Nina means is that you *shouldn't* do that. Hitting never solves anything. We have to figure out how to solve our problems in a better way. That's why Mr. Morton wants us to have D and D time."

"You could help us with something else," Nina admitted to Ozzy. "Tell us why Calliope has been acting so weird."

Ozzy shrugged. "I don't know much about Calliope. Edgar might know something."

Edgar spent most of his time writing in his journal under a tree in an old picture hanging on the wall. He and his pal Nate liked writing scary stories.

Cassidy marched to the back of the room and tapped a pencil on the chipped frame. Edgar and Nate both oozed out of the picture.

Edgar adjusted his crooked glasses. "This better be important," he said.

Nate nodded. He usually didn't have much to say. "We were at a scary part in our story," he explained softly.

"We need to know about Calliope," Nina said.

"What she was like when she first moved to Sleepy Hollow," added Jeff.

"We never met her and her cat before you brought her to our classroom. We heard things about them, though," Edgar said, opening his journal to the very front. "I wrote about them here."

Edgar started to read from the yellowed pages of his journal. "'A new girl has come to Sleepy Hollow to live at the Blackburn Mansion with her uncle. She is the heir to the Rockstone Railroad fortune.'"

Green diamonds floated in the air around Edgar as Sadie appeared and shivered. "That poor girl had to live with her uncle Bartholomew."

"Everyone knew how mean he was," Ozzy said. "Kids avoided him."

"Nobody visited the new girl," Sadie moaned. "So sad. So sad."

Edgar nodded. "Bartholomew's son, Julian, was the worst bully Sleepy Hollow ever did see."

Jeff found it hard to believe there had been a bully worse than Andrew or Ozzy.

21

"Julian was rotten. Spoiled rotten," Ozzy huffed.

"They didn't have to go to school," Edgar explained. "They had their own teacher who taught them reading and ciphering and all."

"I met Julian once," Nate whispered, "at the County Fair. I showed him the big blue marble Pa gave me for my birthday. Right after that, my one and only marble went missing. I'm sure Julian stole it."

Edgar's ghostly face turned three shades of red behind his glasses. "That horrible boy. He had plenty of money. He could've bought a wagonload of marbles, but he stole your most prized possession!"

Nate nodded. "Julian was just like his father. When he wanted something, he would stop at nothing to get it."

Edgar snapped his journal shut. "That's all we know," he told Cassidy, Nina, and Jeff. "Except that folks told of Calliope's treasure hidden somewhere in Sleepy Hollow."

"There isn't much to go on," Jeff said.

"It would make a good story, though," Edgar said, his eyes lighting up.

"Let's do it!" Nate agreed. The two friends zipped back in the picture to write.

Sadie floated in front of Jeff. Long stringy hair nearly covered her gray face. "I know about unhappy. I will do anything . . . anything at all . . . to help Calliope."

5
Marshmallow King

In the lunchroom the next day, Andrew plopped his sack lunch on the table next to Jeff's, even though there wasn't enough room. Everyone had to squish together so Andrew could sit down.

"I have the bestest lunch at this table," Andrew bragged.

"You mean the best," Nina said, correcting Andrew's grammar.

"That's what I said," Andrew snapped.

Cassidy rolled her eyes.

Jeff sat up straight and opened his lunchbox. "I doubt it," Jeff said. "Nobody makes pimento cheese sandwiches like my dad."

"Who cares about *poop*-mento sandwiches," Andrew said, "when you can have these?" He pulled out an entire bag of MegaMarshmallows.

Carla shook her finger at Andrew. "That's not . . ."

". . . a healthy lunch," Darla finished.

For once, Cassidy had to agree with the twins. "That's like eating a bagful of sugar," she said.

Andrew shook his head and grinned. "No, it isn't," he said. "MegaMarshmallows are funner than sugar."

"You mean more fun," Nina corrected.

"Like I said," Andrew continued. "Funner. I bet I can stuff more marshmallows in my mouth than anyone at this table."

"Can not," Jeff said without thinking.

"Can too," Andrew blurted.

"Can't," Jeff said.

"Can." Andrew slapped his hand on the table. "And I'll prove it."

"Don't listen to him!" Nina pleaded with Jeff, but it was too late. Jeff wasn't about to let Andrew prove he was better at anything.

One by one, the boys poked marsh-mallows into their mouths. Soon, their cheeks made them look like deranged chipmunks. Still, they shoved in more.

Carla squeezed her eyes shut. "This is so . . ."

". . . disgusting," Darla said, her own eyes wide open.

"Both of you stop it before someone chokes," Cassidy warned them.

Andrew acted like he didn't hear a word. He jammed another marshmallow in his mouth.

Jeff grabbed the bag. That's when Andrew reached under Jeff's arm and tickled him.

"*AAAAHHHHHHHHHH!*" Jeff couldn't help but scream. When he did, gooey marshmallows exploded from his mouth all over the table. They plopped on lunch trays. They plunked into milk cartons. They stuck to Carla's and Darla's hair.

Carla jumped up from the table. "You are in so much . . ."

"... trouble," Darla said. They marched off to get Mr. Morton.

Andrew didn't look the least bit bothered. "I won," he said, pumping his arm in the air. "I am the MegaMarshmallow King!"

"More like a marshmallow nut," Nina said as she plucked a soggy lump from her T-shirt.

Jeff was ready to whack Andrew over the head with his pimento cheese sandwich, but Andrew started dancing around

the table. "The bestest, the bestest," he sang. "I am the bestest."

"Ignore him," Nina told Jeff.

But to Jeff, ignoring Andrew was impossible.

That afternoon, right before the end of the school day, Jeff hurried to get a drink of water before Mr. Morton started Drama and Debate. Cassidy and Nina followed him into the hallway. All the other kids stayed inside the classroom. "I have to hurry so I can go first," Jeff told

Cassidy when she tried to keep him in the hallway.

"Forget about Andrew for a minute," Nina told Jeff.

"Andrew?" a voice bellowed. Green air swirled over the water fountain until Ozzy took full form. "Where is that rotten kid?"

"Why do you care?" Nina asked.

Ozzy puffed up his chest until he looked like he might pop. "I rule this class-room and I am the best at every-thing," Ozzy told her. "Nobody dares to go against me. That Andrew kid doesn't know when to stop."

"You're just jealous because he's better at bullying than you are." That came from Becky. She popped into view and stuck her finger at Ozzy. Nina shivered when Becky's finger went all the way through her brother's chest.

"Nobody is better than me," Ozzy said. "At anything! I'll prove it. Now, where is that boy?"

Ozzy didn't have a chance to prove anything because, just then, the kids heard a clinking sound on the steps leading down from the rest of the school. Or maybe it was a clanking sound. Ozzy and Becky popped out of sight as Olivia reached the bottom step.

"Thought I heard some voices," Olivia said. "I told Rupert we should check it out."

Cassidy, Jeff, and Nina stared at the rooster cradled in Olivia's arms. Olivia had been Sleepy Hollow's custodian since before most of the kids' parents could remember. She had a laugh that was as big as her heart. She was known for taking care of sick animals until they were healthy and ready for good homes. She didn't only care for cute little kitties and puppies. She also took care of lizards, snakes, and even roosters, like Rupert.

Rupert flapped his wings and crowed. "That's just like Rupert," Olivia said with a wink. "He's always crowing about something. Thinks he's got important things to say, I suppose. That's why I'm trying to find him a new home. He did

so much crowing, the neighbors complained. Crowing will do that, you know. Make people mad."

Cassidy, Nina, and Jeff stared at Rupert and nodded.

"A little less crowing and a little more cooperation would solve old Rupert's problem." Olivia spoke so loud her voice boomed to the farthest corners of the hallway. "We'd do well to remember that. All of us! Now, every last one of you better scoot into class. Looks like D and D time has already started. Wonder what Andrew is so excited about."

"No!" Jeff yelled. He turned and raced into the classroom, forgetting all about Ozzy, Olivia, and Rupert. There was only one thing on his mind. Beating Andrew.

6
No Trespassing

Jeff was too late. Andrew stood dead center at the front of the classroom, talking about the Blackburn Estate AGAIN. "My mother said I can have anything I want in my new room," Andrew bragged.

Nina rolled her eyes in Cassidy's direction as they hurried to their seats.

Calliope walked in slow circles around Andrew. She pulled her hair and her mouth opened as if she needed air. Her cat, Cocomo, trotted alongside her. Around and around they paced, but Andrew didn't see a thing.

Jeff raised his hand. "Can I go next, Mr. Morton?"

Mr. Morton gently shook his head. "You know better than to interrupt. You should be listening to Andrew."

"Yeah," Andrew said. "Listen to all the cool stuff I get. Maybe, if you're really nice to me, I'll let you see some of it."

Jeff's face burned red, and he slumped down in his chair.

That's when Ozzy, Becky, and their friend Sadie popped into view. Ozzy couldn't stand that Andrew was getting so much attention, but Ozzy couldn't do anything about it because Calliope was in his way. All three ghosts got in line behind Calliope and paraded in circles around Andrew.

Andrew bragged on and on. "The best part," he said, "is that Dad is going to tear down those old stinky stables and build a skateboard ramp just for me."

At that, Calliope stopped pacing. So did Cocomo. The cat grew to the size of a tiger and hissed right into Andrew's face. Calliope shook her head and grabbed for Andrew's neck, but her hands passed right through the boy.

Giant goose bumps covered Andrew's

arms and his teeth chattered with a shiver.

Cassidy gasped. Nina whimpered. Even Jeff's face grew pale. Ozzy, Becky, and Sadie flew around Calliope. "Stop!" they moaned. "Stop, stop, stop!"

Calliope didn't hear them. She reached for Andrew again, but just then, the bell rang, ending the school day.

Kids jumped up from their seats and Andrew hurried to be first in line. Cassidy, Nina, and Jeff stared at Calliope. Then they turned to each other. "We have to do something," Nina said quietly. "We can't let her suffer anymore."

Cassidy agreed. "I don't like Andrew that much, but we can't let Calliope hurt him."

That afternoon, on the way home, Cassidy pulled her friends into the shadows of the old trees that lined the long drive to the Blackburn Estate.

"I figured something out," Cassidy said. "Calliope's problem has to do with the Blackburn Estate."

"The Blackburn Estate is everyone's problem," Jeff sputtered. "It has been ever since Andrew started bragging about it."

"For the last time," Nina said, "forget about Andrew."

"Maybe not entirely," Cassidy said.

"What?" Nina and Jeff asked at the same time.

"We have to help Calliope find her voice," Cassidy said. "Andrew might be able to help."

"Andrew does a lot of mean things," Nina said, "but I'm pretty sure he hasn't done anything to Calliope. He doesn't even know the ghosts exist!"

"Every time Andrew starts talking during D and D time, Calliope gets very upset," Cassidy explained.

"Andrew's talking upsets everybody," Jeff pointed out.

"Calliope lived at the Blackburn Estate," Nina said, ignoring Jeff. "Maybe she's homesick."

"Or maybe she wants to warn us about the Blackburn Estate," Cassidy said slowly.

Jeff's eyes grew wide, and he jumped six inches in the air, as if someone had poked him awake. "You might be on to something," he said. "In the movie, *No Body's Home*, a ghost tried to warn a married couple about a gas leak before

the house exploded. The ghost acted crazy."

"What could Calliope be trying to tell us about at the Blackburn Estate?" Nina asked.

"Maybe if we did a little exploring, we could find a clue," Cassidy said.

Jeff pointed up the driveway. A fence had been built across it and a sign said NO TRESPASSING. "We can't even get close to the house. There's no way to find out anything."

Cassidy thought for a full minute. "There is one way," Cassidy told Jeff. "But you're definitely not going to like it."

7
Ghost Parade

"We have to get Andrew to take us on a tour of the Blackburn Mansion," Cassidy suggested.

"No way!" Jeff argued. "Andrew will never stop bragging if we act interested."

"It's the only way to get inside that house," Nina said.

Cassidy nodded. "If you act like you want to go, Andrew will take us in a second."

Jeff thought, and he thought hard. But he couldn't think of a better idea.

The next afternoon when it was his turn for D and D, Jeff tried to ignore the four ghosts hovering in the classroom. Calliope stood with her mouth open and Cocomo scratched at her owner's leg.

Ozzy buzzed around Andrew's head while Sadie patted Calliope's shoulder.

Jeff took a deep breath, looked right at Andrew, and said, "I think Andrew is making up the story about buying the Blackburn Estate."

Andrew jumped up from his seat. "I didn't make it up!" he yelled. Andrew's head bumped into Ozzy, but Andrew was too mad to notice anything unusual. Ozzy went flying through the air and halfway through a bookshelf before he finally came to a stop.

Mr. Morton held up his hand to quiet the boys while Jeff crossed his arms over his chest. "Then prove it," Jeff dared.

Andrew puffed out his chest. "No problem. I'll give you a personal tour."

"Just me?" Jeff asked. "That wouldn't prove anything. If the Estate really belongs to your family, you could invite everyone."

Nina nodded, but Carla looked shocked. "It's not polite . . ."

"... to invite yourself," Darla finished.

"All right," Andrew said, looking around the room. "Everyone here is invited on a private tour of the Blackburn Estate."

Mr. Morton cleared his throat. "Andrew might need to check with his parents before doing that."

Andrew shook his head. "No problem. My mom always wants me to bring friends home."

Jeff felt guilty for a minute. Andrew

had invited Jeff over lots of times, but he had never gone. "It's settled, then," Jeff said with a smile. "Everyone who can, will go to the Blackburn Estate after school today."

Ozzy's eyes got big. He danced with Sadie and Calliope. "We get to go to the Blackburn Estate. We get to go!"

Nina stared in horror and mouthed the word "No!"

After the bell rang, Nina, Jeff, and Cassidy were the last kids in the classroom. Jeff shook his head at Ozzy. "You can't go with us," Jeff explained.

Ozzy's eyebrows grew five times bigger as he frowned. "We were invited!" he yelled. "You heard Andrew. He said everybody could go."

"It would be rude not to go," Sadie said softly.

"But you'll fade to nothing," Jeff argued. "You need to bring something that belongs to you."

The kids had found out that the ghosts

were trapped in the basement unless something belonging to them went along.

Sadie pointed to the necklace that she had given to Nina a while ago. Nina touched the gold heart that hung around her neck.

Ozzy pointed to Cassidy's backpack. "We know what's in there," he said. Cassidy's face turned red. A piece of wood from Ozzy's old desk was in the front pocket of her backpack. Ozzy had used the splintered wood from his desk to go upstairs and explore. He caused so much trouble the kids decided to keep the splinter hidden.

Jeff shrugged. "Maybe Calliope and Cocomo should go, too." He grabbed Calliope's violin and Cocomo's dish and stuffed them into his backpack.

The three kids started up the back staircase followed by their ghostly friends. Ozzy's ghost sister, Becky, flew up behind Ozzy. "Where are you going?" she shrieked.

"Out!" Ozzy said simply.

"I want to go!!!" Becky wailed.

"You cannot go," Ozzy teased. "You weren't in the room when Andrew invited us."

Nina, Jeff, and Cassidy heard Becky's moans as the kids went out into the sunlight. Andrew was already leading Mr. Morton and a group of third graders down the sidewalk.

Jeff looked at Cassidy and Nina. "Get ready for a ghost parade," he said. "I just hope we're not walking into a big mistake."

8
The Blackburn Estate

The Blackburn Mansion loomed ahead. Dark storm clouds blanketed the sun, casting the grounds into deep shadows. Wind knocked through the dead branches of a tree and sounded like knuckles cracking. Thunder rumbled in the distance. No one spoke as most of the kids from the third-grade classroom, Mr. Morton, and four ghosts paraded up the tree-lined drive.

Carla whispered as they got closer. "It's big and . . ."

". . . dark," Darla said with a gulp.

No one argued with the twins. Leafless limbs from a giant tree reached out like a claw toward the huge old house. Many windows were boarded up, but a crew of workers banged away at the roof.

Mr. Morton cleared his throat. "With a fresh coat of paint, I'm sure it will be magnificent."

Calliope seemed to agree. She fluttered past the kids and oozed through the closed wooden door. Cocomo, Ozzy, and Sadie followed her.

"Wait until you see the front hall," Andrew told his teacher. "You could fit two schools inside it."

Andrew led the way up the crumbling steps and across the squeaking boards of the porch. The heavy iron handle creaked as Andrew pulled open the massive door.

Everyone huddled together within the shadows of the front hallway. Nina wondered where the ghosts had gone.

Andrew pointed up the long wooden staircase. A dusty blood-red carpet covered the steps. "When my parents aren't

looking, I slide down that railing. It's fun."

Jeff didn't pay any attention to the fancy stairs. All he noticed were the ancient portraits. The eyes of the people in the paintings seemed to be watching him just like the last time he was there. Something wasn't right, and goose bumps broke out on his arms.

"Come on," Andrew said. "I'll show you where the game room will be. We're tearing out the old library. There's going to be a pool table and a big-screen TV."

Jeff started after the group until something made him turn around. He was sure someone was following him, but when he looked, no one was there.

Nina and Cassidy hung back from the group, too. Nina whispered to her friends, "What happened to the ghosts?"

"I hope we haven't lost them," Cassidy admitted. "Becky would never forgive us if we didn't bring Ozzy back."

"If only getting rid of a ghost was that easy," Jeff reminded her. He looked around at the peeling paint on the walls, and shrugged. "They must be around here somewhere."

Cassidy shuddered. "This place gives me the creeps."

"You feel it, too?" Jeff asked.

"Feel what?" Cassidy and Nina asked together.

Jeff leaned close to his two friends, and whispered, "Something, or someone, is following us."

9
Dead End

A bolt of lightning electrified the room with blinding light for no longer than a second. It was long enough for Nina to catch a glimpse of something in the cracked mirror.

"*AAAAHHHHHHHH!*"

When Nina yelled, Cassidy fell back into Jeff. Jeff stumbled and fell flat on the floor. "Why'd you scream?" Jeff snapped as he pulled himself up and wiped off the seat of his pants.

"It was only lightning," Cassidy added.

Nina pointed a trembling finger at the mantel. The mirror above the fireplace was cracked and stained. "I . . . I . . . I saw something in there," Nina stammered.

Jeff rolled his eyes. "It was your reflection," he said, "so I understand why you were scared."

"Very funny," Nina said, but she wasn't laughing. Then she said something else, but her words were lost in a clap of thunder so strong it rattled the windows and shook the floor beneath the kids' sneakers.

Cassidy patted Nina on the shoulder. "Jeff is right. There's nothing in this room except us."

"Tell that to Cocomo," Nina said. Nina's voice trembled, and she sounded as if she might cry.

Cocomo darted into the hallway and arched her back. When she hissed at the mirror, her fangs glistened. Calliope floated into the room, followed by Sadie and Ozzy.

"There you are," Cassidy said. "We were wondering what happened to you."

"Don't take off like that," Jeff warned the ghosts, "or you might be left behind."

Getting left behind was the last thing on the ghosts' minds just then. Another bolt of lightning cracked open the sky. When it did, Cassidy saw what had scared Cocomo and Nina. Cassidy grabbed Jeff's T-shirt and dragged him away from the mirror when a very big man appeared in the smudged glass.

"It's Bartholomew," Ozzy gasped. "Bartholomew Blackburn."

Bartholomew's face was wrinkly yellow, and a black curly beard covered his chin. His bushy eyebrows formed a thick line over his dark narrow eyes. He

opened his mouth and boomed, "I want what is rightfully mine!"

The words created a rush of wind that knocked Ozzy and Sadie clear through the walls. Cassidy, Jeff, and Nina clung to each other as they tried to remain standing.

"Mine! Mine!" a second voice taunted from what seemed like every corner of the room.

"Nooooooo," Sadie cried as she popped back out of the wall. "I know that voice. It belongs to Julian!"

Cocomo slashed through the air with her claws as Bartholomew's arm pushed through the mirror and into the room above the kids' heads. He pointed a finger straight at Calliope.

Calliope opened her mouth as if to scream, but she made no sound.

"Give it to me!" Bartholomew roared. "I want it NOW!"

The last word rose above the thunder and shook the earth. Nina whimpered

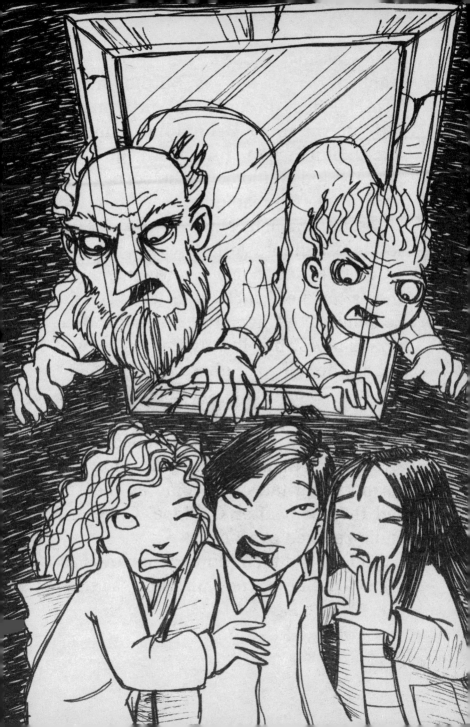

and Cassidy closed her eyes. Jeff grabbed his friends as Bartholomew's form pushed through the dirty mirror and into the room. Behind him came his son. Julian licked his ghostly lips and eyed the kids huddled in the corner.

"Run!" Jeff screamed.

Cassidy ran left. Nina ran right. They both crashed into Jeff.

Calliope had backed away from the ghosts of her uncle and evil cousin. Cocomo raked her claws through their hazy shapes, but it only caused a brief tear in the fabric of ghostly air.

"Look," Jeff said, shaking Cassidy's arm. "Calliope is escaping."

"Follow that ghost!" Nina yelled.

Cassidy, Nina, and Jeff ran after the disappearing tail of Cocomo as they all fled the room after Calliope. Ozzy and Sadie zoomed overhead.

Calliope led them down a narrow passageway. She turned through a short doorway that the kids had to duck to pass through. They found themselves in a dark hallway filled with cobwebs. That opened into a hallway that was so dark the flash of lightning bolts could not reach it. Calliope led them deeper and deeper into the Blackburn Mansion.

"I'm so turned around I'll never find my way out again," Nina whimpered. "We'll be trapped in here with hundreds of spiders." Nina hated spiders more than anything.

"Don't worry," Jeff said. "Calliope knows her way. She used to live here."

"But where is she taking us?" Cassidy gasped.

"Ours, ours," came Julian's voice from somewhere behind them.

"Wherever it is, she'd better hurry," Jeff said through gritted teeth, "because Julian and his father are closing in fast."

Just then, the passageway they had followed came to a dead end at a heavy door. Calliope and Cocomo slipped right through the door. Jeff, Cassidy, and Nina skidded to a stop. "Do we dare open it?" Nina asked.

"We have to," Cassidy said.

Jeff nodded. "One. Two. Three. Open!"

10
Secret Compartment

The door jerked from Jeff's hand as a gust of wind blew it back. Rain pelted the kids' faces and lightning seared through the sky.

"This is the back door of the mansion," Nina gasped.

"Where did Calliope go?" Cassidy yelled over rumbling thunder.

"I WANT WHAT IS MINE!" boomed Bartholomew's voice from behind.

"Mine, mine," Julian repeated.

"Do something," Nina yelped. "Before Bartholomew gets us!"

Rain fell in slanted sheets across the yard of weeds, and wind bent nearby trees until they looked like they might snap.

"There!" Cassidy yelled. "Calliope is going into that old building."

"Quick," Jeff said. "We have to get to her before Bartholomew catches up to us."

Wind blew them first one way, then another. Rain drenched their clothes. Ozzy and Sadie somersaulted in the wind, screeching with effort as they followed Cassidy, Jeff, and Nina. Lightning cracked a nearby tree as the kids and their ghostly companions finally reached the old stables, where they had last seen Calliope heading.

The smell of dust and straw made Nina sneeze when they pulled open the door and crept inside.

"Calliope?" Cassidy yelled into the shadows of the stables. "Where are you?"

"WHERE ARE YOU?" bellowed another voice.

It was Bartholomew.

"Where? Where?" Julian asked.

Calliope floated out from a stall. She pulled at her stringy wet hair. Cocomo leapt through the air to claw at Bartholomew, but she soared straight through Calliope's uncle.

Bartholomew didn't pay attention to the angry cat. He didn't look at Cassidy, Jeff, or Nina. Instead, he swelled in size until he filled the door-way. Bartholomew spoke to Calliope. "You should not have returned. Now there will be no escape."

"No escape. No escape," Julian repeated.

Calliope shook her head, her hair whipping back and forth. Ozzy and Sadie shrank to the size of puppets and hid from Bartholomew under a pile of straw.

"Where is it hidden?" Bartholomew demanded of Calliope. "Give it to me. No one here can protect you."

"No one. No one," Julian added.

Calliope opened her mouth but still

couldn't speak. She nodded to a small board near the base of the corner stall.

Jeff understood that Calliope was trying to tell them something. He hurried to pry up the loose board and found a secret compartment.

Uncle Bartholomew roared, "Finally. Your hiding place is revealed!"

"The treasure! The treasure!" Julian yelled.

Ozzy scattered straw as he flew through the air. "You mean the stories of hidden treasure are true? TRUE! Let me at it!"

The three kids held their breath as Jeff pulled out a brown packet from the secret compartment. Before Jeff could look inside the package, Julian snatched it from Jeff and flew off to the rafters with it.

"NO!" screamed Calliope.

11
Treasure

"Did someone say treasure?" Andrew said. Mr. Morton and the rest of the class followed Andrew into the stables.

Jeff quickly explained, "There's a legend about hidden treasure here on the property. That's what we're looking for."

"Then it's my treasure now!" Andrew squealed. "Where is it?"

"In a brown bag," Cassidy told her classmates. "It's somewhere in the stable."

"I'll find it first!" Andrew snapped.

Mr. Morton shrugged his shoulders. "We might as well have a treasure hunt until the rain slows down."

Andrew, Mr. Morton, and the rest of the kids headed off to search the back rooms of the stables.

Jeff looked up to the rafters. Julian had ripped open the brown bag and dumped the bag and its contents onto the floor.

"Letters?" Julian shrieked. "These are nothing but letters!"

Uncle Bartholomew dove inside the bag and flew out empty-handed. "Where is the treasure?" he howled.

Calliope concentrated hard and scooped the several pieces of yellowed paper from the floor. "These ARE my treasure," she said. "I was unable to speak since I

promised my friend never to tell where they were hidden, but I could not let them be destroyed."

Cassidy handed Calliope the rest of the letters. "These are notes from somebody named Amy."

Calliope nodded. "She was my friend. My only friend. When we couldn't sneak time to be together, we left secret messages in hiding places around the estate."

"No treasure?" Julian gasped, holding a plump hand to his chest.

"Friendship IS a treasure," Nina said bravely.

Julian and Uncle Bartholomew moaned and groaned. Nina put her hands over her ears to block out the horrible noise.

"Stop it!" Nina screamed, but they only moaned more. They swirled around and around and moaned even louder. Everything in the room swirled with them, including the kids.

"It's the end of the world!" Cassidy screamed.

Jeff, Nina, and Cassidy closed their eyes and hugged one another tightly.

"What's going on?" Mr. Morton asked the kids as he hurried back from the tack room. "We heard yelling."

Nina, Jeff, and Cassidy dropped into a pile of straw. Andrew and the rest of the class stood behind their teacher. Uncle Bartholomew and Julian were nowhere to be seen.

"I think they're scared of a little thunder and rain," Andrew teased. "It must be a bunny storm." He knew that Jeff once jumped at a picture of a rabbit appearing suddenly on a computer screen.

Mr. Morton frowned at Andrew and said, "I think the sun is coming out. We'd better go home. Thank you for the tour, Andrew."

The kids and their teacher headed out of the stable, leaving Andrew behind. A few drops of rain continued to plop on the gravel road, but the sun peeked through the dark clouds.

Jeff, Nina, and Cassidy waited until everyone else was a good distance away before Jeff whispered, "What happened to Uncle Bartholomew and Cousin Julian?"

Cassidy shrugged. "Maybe they left. Without the treasure, their reason for remaining at the estate is gone."

"Or maybe they're looking for another treasure," Nina said with a shudder.

The gravel crunched under the kids' feet as they stepped into the fresh air. Nina smiled at Sadie, Calliope, Cocomo, and Ozzy. "At least things will be back to normal at school now. Well, as normal as Ghostville Elementary can be."

Jeff shook his head. "I can't believe we risked our necks for a bunch of letters."

"Shhh," Cassidy said, "here comes Andrew."

Andrew ran up behind the three friends. "I have to stop my dad from tearing anything down or else the treasure might be lost forever. I'll tell Dad to fix up the old place. That'll give me the chance to search the Blackburn Estate from top to bottom. Jeff, will you help me find that treasure?"

"Me?" Jeff asked, surprised.

"Sure," Andrew said. "The two of us will be a treasure-hunting team."

Jeff looked at Cassidy and Nina. Ozzy, Calliope, and Sadie floated beside them. "Only if my other friends can help, too," Jeff said.

Andrew shrugged. "Sure, you're all invited."

"All of us?" Nina said, glancing up at the ghosts.

"The more, the merrier," Andrew said.

Jeff laughed as Andrew walked away. "Even if there isn't a treasure, the Blackburn Estate will be fun to explore," Jeff said.

Calliope didn't say a word as she hugged the letters close to her chest. She only dropped one. Nina picked it up and

put it in her pocket so it wouldn't get lost.

She put her arms around Jeff and Cassidy. "Calliope is right," Nina said. "There is no greater treasure than friends, and you guys are the greatest treasure ever!"

Ready for more spooky fun?
Then take a sneak peek at the next

Ghostville Elementary®

#11 The Treasure Haunt

"This is the worst idea of Mr. Morton's yet," Andrew complained and threw a green sleeping bag beside his desk. "It's bad enough we have to go to school during the day, but spending the night is a stupid idea."

"I think it's a great idea," Cassidy told him. "Our classroom could win the best computer ever made, so you better get over your complaining and start reading. I don't see any stickers by your name."

Cassidy pointed to the poster behind their teacher's desk. Cassidy's name had ten stickers by it, one for each book she had read. Jeff and Nina each had eight. Carla and Darla had the most, with fifteen stickers each. There wasn't a single star next to Andrew's name.

"It sure would be nice if every class could get a new computer," Nina said as she set her backpack and sleeping bag next to her desk.

Andrew dumped his backpack on the floor as more kids filed into the room. "I think it would be nice if every classroom got boarded up and we never had to go to school again," Andrew told her.

Carla and her twin sister, Darla, skipped into the room. Carla stopped when she heard Andrew, and nodded. "This room used to be . . ."

". . . boarded up," Darla finished. "But that's when people thought . . ."

". . . it was haunted," Carla said.

"Nobody believes those silly stories," Andrew said. "Do they?"

Nina and Cassidy stared at the air above Andrew. Ozzy floated there, plucking a stray hair out of Andrew's head.

"Ouch!" Andrew yelped and swatted his head. He swirled around and glared at the twins. "Who did that?"

"Not me," Carla and Darla said.

Cassidy giggled, but nobody heard her because their teacher bustled in, rubbing his hands together. "Hurry," Mr. Morton said. "Everyone find a space to read and sleep. We'll have pizza in an hour."

"Head for the back," Cassidy told Nina and Jeff. "Before Andrew beats us."

Jeff hurried to the back of the room and set up a small pup tent. The class settled in for a long night of reading. Everyone, of course, except the ghosts. They were gearing up for a night full of haunting. Especially Ozzy.

The longer Ozzy watched, the more

steamed he got about the kids invading the classroom at night. Literally. Smoke started coming out of his nose and ears. Smoke seeped out of his head.

Carla stopped fluffing her pillow to sniff. "Call 911! Something . . ."

". . . is burning!" her twin sister, Darla, yelled.

"Calm down," Mr. Morton told the class. "I'm sure everything is fine. Keep reading while I check on it."

When Mr. Morton stepped into the hallway, Andrew tossed a paper wad at Carla.

Carla gave him a dirty look. "Just wait until . . ."

". . . Mr. Morton gets back," Darla finished for her.

Andrew hopped up from his sleeping bag and put his hands on his hips. "Just wait until Mr. Morton gets back," he said in a whiny voice. He stuck his nose in the air and wiggled his hips.

Cassidy didn't like Andrew's teasing,

but she couldn't help smiling at the silly way Andrew jiggled his hips.

Not Ozzy. Ozzy didn't like Andrew getting all the attention. Ozzy was used to being the biggest bully in the basement classroom. He stopped steaming and jumped into Andrew's sleeping bag.

Cassidy gasped. What was Ozzy up to?

About the Authors

Marcia Thornton Jones and Debbie Dadey got into the *spirit* of writing when they worked together at the same school in Lexington, Kentucky. Since then, Debbie has *haunted* several states. She currently *haunts* Ft. Collins, CO, with her three children, two dogs, and husband. Marcia remains in Lexington, KY, where she lives with her husband and two cats. Debbie and Marcia have fun with spooky stories. They have scared themselves silly with *The Adventures of the Bailey School Kids* and *The Bailey City Monsters* series.

MORE SERIES YOU'LL LOVE

Abracadabra!

The members of the Abracadabra Club have a few tricks up their sleeves—and a few tricks you can learn to do yourself!

A JIGSAW JONES MYSTERY

Jigsaw and his partner, Mila, know that mysteries are like jigsaw puzzles—you've got to look at all the pieces to solve the case!

THE SECRETS OF DROON
by TONY ABBOTT

Time for a magic carpet ride! Join Eric, Julie, and Neal on their wild adventures as they help Princess Keeah save the secret, magical world of Droon.

www.scholastic.com/kids

LITTLE APPLE

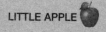

What's Buried in the Basement?

From the authors of THE BAILEY SCHOOL KIDS™!

Marcia Thornton Jones & Debbie Dadey

Ghostville Elementary®

The Treasure Haunt

■SCHOLASTIC

The kids abandon their all-night read-a-thon to search for treasure. But the Sleepy Hollow Elementary ghosts have plans of their own... like turning the hunt-a-thon into a haunt-a-thon!

www.scholastic.com

■SCHOLASTIC